JPIC Fireen
The fire engine book /
34028086393072
ALD $3.99
10/08/14

IRE ENG.

3 4028 08639 3072
HARRIS COUNTY PUBLIC LIBRARY

Tik

D1261451

A GOLDEN BOOK • NEW YORK

Copyright © 1950, 1959, renewed 1987 by Random House, Inc. All rights reserved. Published in the United States by Golden Books, an imprint of Random House Children's Books, a division of Random House, Inc., New York. Originally published in 1950 by Simon and Schuster, Inc., and Artists and Writers Guild, Inc. Golden Books, A Golden Book, A Little Golden Book, the G colophon, and the distinctive gold spine are registered trademarks of Random House, Inc. A Little Golden Book Classic is a trademark of Random House, Inc.

www.goldenbooks.com
www.randomhouse.com/kids
Educators and librarians, for a variety of teaching tools, visit us at www.randomhouse.com/teachers
Library of Congress Control Number: 00-109707
ISBN: 978-0-307-96024-5
Printed in the United States of America
40 39 38 37 36 35
Random House Children's Books supports the First Amendment and celebrates the right to read.

Ding, ding, ding! goes the alarm.

The firemen slide down the pole.

Clang, clang, clang! goes the fire engine bell.

The chief is on his way.

Here they come!

Watch out! Make way for the hose car.

Hurry, hurry! Jump on the hook-and-ladder truck!

The people come running out to see

the great big hook-and-ladder truck.

Here they are at the fire.

The chief tells his men what to do.

Quick! Connect the hoses!

S-s-s-s! goes the water.

Crank, crank. Up go the ladders.

Up go the firemen with their hoses.

Chop, chop, chop! go the axes.

Crash! go the windows.

Down the ladders come the firemen.

They jump into the net to save things from the fire!

Sput, sput, sput! Out goes the fire.

Tired firemen and people go home.

Harris County Public Library, Houston, TX

Hurray for the brave firemen!